WHEN THE PIGS TOOK OVER

by **ARTHUR DORROS**

illustrated by **DIANE GREENSEID**

DUTTON CHILDREN'S BOOKS · NEW YORK

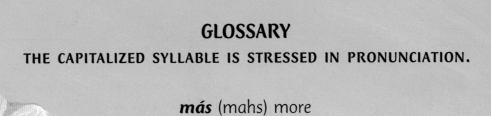

GLOSSARY
THE CAPITALIZED SYLLABLE IS STRESSED IN PRONUNCIATION.

más (mahs) more

magnífico (mahg-NEE-fee-coh) magnificent

caracoles (cahr-ah-COH-lehs) snails

¿Qué hacemos? (kay ah-SEH-mohs) What should we do?

pájaros (PAH-hah-rohs) birds

puercos (PWEHR-cohs) pigs

música (MOO-see-cah) music

sí (see) yes

Text copyright © 2002 by Arthur Dorros
Illustrations copyright © 2002 by Diane Greenseid

CIP Data is available.

Published in the United States 2002 by Dutton Children's Books,
a division of Penguin Putnam Books for Young Readers
345 Hudson Street, New York, New York 10014
www.penguinputnam.com

Designed by Alan Carr & Amy Berniker
Printed in Hong Kong
First Edition
ISBN 0-525-42030-4
1 3 5 7 9 10 8 6 4 2

For Cailin and Reilly
—A.D.

For Joan and her violin
—D.G.

Alonzo was little.
Don Carlos was big.
He was Alonzo's big brother—
much older and much, much bigger.

Alonzo had one hat.
Don Carlos had seven,
and he wore them all at once.
"*Más,*" said Don Carlos
as he found three more.
Oh no, thought Alonzo. More.

When Alonzo ate one ice-cream cone,
Don Carlos ate four—
vanilla, chocolate, pineapple, and coconut.
"*Más*," he said. He wanted more.
He wanted to try Alonzo's ice cream, too.

Don Carlos had lots of ideas about "more,"
especially at his restaurant.
Don Carlos had the only restaurant
in the village.
He served huge, sizzling, steaming
plates of food, bowls of food,
platters of food that people liked eating.
"¿Más?" Don Carlos always asked.

Alonzo liked playing his violin at the restaurant—
ZEEOH, ZEEAH.
"¡Magnífico!" villagers cheered.
Of all the villagers, none could
play music as well as Alonzo.
Alonzo said it was because
he played the violin almost all the time.
"Más," said Don Carlos.

People were happily listening to the music
and eating.
But Don Carlos was thinking about more foods
that he could add to the restaurant menu.

Alonzo read that in a big, fancy
restaurant in the city, people ate snails.
"¡Caracoles!" said Don Carlos. Snails!

There were lots of snails in the village.
Alonzo helped gather snails.
Soon there were pails of snails, baskets
of snails, wheelbarrows of snails.
"*Más*," said Don Carlos.
They looked for more snails.

Snails crawled out of baskets, pails,
and wheelbarrows in the restaurant kitchen.
The snails were looking for food.

They ate vegetables
in the kitchen and
flowers off the tables.

The snails ate and ate—and ate.
They ate every blade of grass,
every plant and flower in the village.
"¿Qué hacemos?" the villagers cried,
wondering what to do.

"¡*Pájaros!*" Alonzo said.
  Birds! He had seen birds eat snails.
  He threw corn and bread crumbs
  to attract birds.
  At first only a few birds landed.
  "*Más*," said Don Carlos.
  The villagers tossed more crumbs.

Birds flapped in tree branches,
fluttered on rooftops,
even landed on people's heads.

The birds started to eat snails.
They raced across roads,
finding snails to eat.

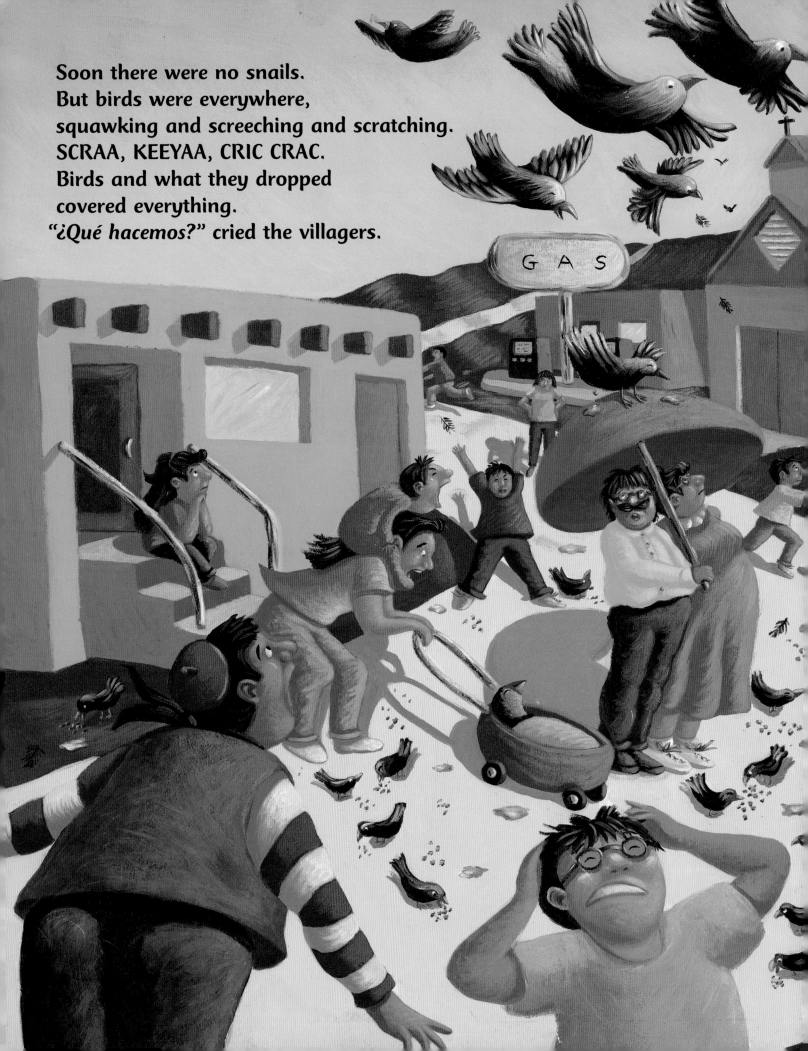

Soon there were no snails.
But birds were everywhere,
squawking and screeching and scratching.
SCRAA, KEEYAA, CRIC CRAC.
Birds and what they dropped
covered everything.
"¿Qué hacemos?" cried the villagers.

"¡*Puercos!*" said Alonzo.
Pigs! He had seen pigs chase birds away.
Alonzo and the villagers rounded up pigs.
Pigs ran, snorting and grunting, at the birds.
GARUMPF, ERRR, ERRR, ERRR.
But the birds kept flapping through the village.
"*Más,*" said Don Carlos.

Alonzo asked Don Carlos if he was sure
he wanted more.
"¡Sí, más!" Don Carlos said.
Large pigs, small pigs,
pigs with spots and pigs with none,
were brought from the nearby countryside.

The pigs snuffled and snapped and squealed.
They scared away the birds
and then began to eat.

They ate everything in front of their snouts.
Pigs clattered into kitchens,

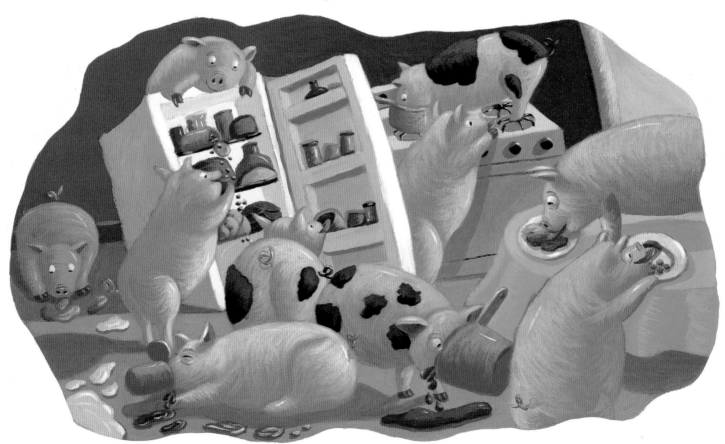

barged into barrels,

trotted into Don Carlos's restaurant, tipped over tables,
tore up the village looking for more.

Don Carlos began to jump and shout,
trying to chase away the pigs.
But the pigs were everywhere.
"¿Qué hacemos?" Everyone wondered what to do.

"¡Música!" Alonzo said.
Music! He had heard a story about a boy who
played music and led rats out of a village.
Alonzo played his violin.
The villagers brought other instruments.
SCRIC, SCRONK, KABLOM, PUM-PAM, PUM-PAM.
Terrible sounds came from the instruments.
The sounds were bad, they were awful,
they were horrible.
The pigs kept running wild.

Don Carlos put his hands over his ears.
The music was more than even he could stand.
"*¡No más!*" he cried.

"¡Más!" Alonzo shouted to the villagers.

The villagers marched through the streets,
playing louder and louder.
Hearing the terrible sounds,
pigs squirmed over and under,
into and around each other, trying to get away.
The pigs ran fast and far,
until there was not a pig in sight.

Don Carlos uncovered his ears.
He looked at how much the village had been destroyed.
"¡No más!" he said sadly.
He realized that more was not always better.

"¡Sí, más!" said Alonzo. He wanted more . . .

practice for the band.
So in the evening, in a cozy village restaurant
that serves a lot but does not serve snails,
a band can be heard playing—or practicing—
more.